Student
Narc

a novel

by

PAUL KROPP

H·I·P Books

HIP Sr. Novels

Library and Archives Canada Cataloguing in Publication

Kropp, Paul, 1948-
    Student narc / Paul Kropp.

(New Series Canada)
ISBN 1-897039-05-0

I. Title. II. Series.

PS8571.R772S87 2004   jC813'.54   C2004-903734-X

General editor: Paul Kropp
Text design: Laura Brady
Illustrations redrawn by: Matt Melanson
Cover design: Robert Corrigan

    3 4 5 6 7   17 16 15 14 13 12

Printed and bound in Canada by Webcom

It wasn't Kevin's idea to start working with the cops. But when his best friend dies from an overdose, somebody has to do something. Kevin finally takes on a whole drug gang – and their boss – in a struggle that leaves him scarred for life.

CHAPTER 1

"Did You Hear?"

I heard about Matt on the way to school, when I was still a little buzzed from the party. It was Squeaky Brown who gave me the word.

"Did you hear?" he asked, with a funny look in his eyes. "Matt's dead."

"Yeah, right," I said, shaking my head. Matt had been with me five, maybe six hours ago. We were both flying pretty high at the time. And he was plenty alive – alive like nobody else in the whole world. That's the way Matt always was.

"I'm not kidding," Squeaky said. He was backing away from me as if he thought I was going to hit him. "I was just over at his place, and the cops are talking to the whole family. I got the word from his brother, and he's really bent out of shape."

"Cut it out, Squeaky. I was with Matt, like, just a couple hours ago," I said, not ready to believe any of this.

"Look, man, how many times do I have to tell you?" Squeaky repeated, staring hard at me. "Matt's dead."

From the look on his face, I finally figured out that Squeaky wasn't kidding. He was trying to tell me straight, and I didn't want to listen.

Squeaky went on, "The word is, Matt took a huge dose of E after the party. Nobody knows where he got it from. It could've been cut with anything, and maybe that's what killed him."

Part of me still couldn't believe what Squeaky had told me. I kept thinking about Matt at the party, about how wild he had been, like most of us, until maybe midnight. Then he dropped some

shrooms – he liked them a lot, but I wouldn't touch those if you paid me. I remember he got really crazy after that. He was up so high that I wondered if he had mixed something else, too.

But I didn't say anything to him. If Squeaky was right – if Matt was dead – maybe I should have.

"Hey, Kevin," Squeaky said as he went off across the road to Matt's high school. Matt and Squeaky both went to the preppy school across the street, the one where the kids got dropped off by mom in the family BMW.

"Yeah?"

"I'm sorry," Squeaky said, "real sorry. I know Matt was, like, your best friend. It shouldn't have been me who had to tell you." Squeaky looked like he wanted to cry or something and was trying hard to hold it back.

I shook my head and walked on to my school – knowledge college, the tech high school. Mine was the school for all the guys who were too tough or too dumb to make it at the preppie high.

"Kevin, did you hear?"

The words came from a bunch of guys hanging

around outside the front doors of my school. I knew what they were going to tell me – and now the truth was sinking in. Now I had to believe it.

"Squeaky told me," I mumbled.

"They found Matt's body on the street," a kid named Birney said. "I don't ever want to go like that. I mean . . . that's dying like a dog."

I looked up just for a second, ready to grab Birney for talking like that about my friend, but he backed down. He wasn't dissing anybody – he was just talking, just shooting his mouth off, like the rest of them. For five, maybe ten minutes, the guys kept on talking, trading rumors, but none of them really knew much. Not as much as I should have known.

The party last night had been nothing special. There were maybe ten of us at the house, doing the same stuff as always. I couldn't remember anyone new coming in at the end of the party, so if Matt died from bad ecstasy, he must have had it with him.

I wasn't watching by then because I was so busy trying to come on to some girl. Besides, I never liked it when Matt was tripping on heavy stuff. I told him that, didn't I? We all told him – but Matt didn't listen. Neither of us was big on listening.

Back when we were litle, Matt was always the guy who took the risks. He liked to live on the edge – risking the falls, daring the cops, mouthing off to teachers. I admired him. He had more guts than me, took more chances, took more falls. Now he'd taken the biggest fall of all, and it didn't make any sense. Sure, Matt did drugs, but he wasn't stupid. He was careful where he got his stuff, and careful how he used it. Until last night, when somehting must have happened.

*   *   *

The school warning bell rang and it was time to go in. The other guys went ahead, but I hung back a little. Somehow the school bell didn't mean much. Matt was dead and I was still alive. Somebody had given my friend the lousy E that had killed him. Somebody had given him stuff that left him dying on the street, alone, cooking in his own skin. I

closed my eyes and tried not to see it in my mind, but I knew … I knew.

I lit up a smoke and leaned back against a fence, thinking about Matt. The two of us had always been tight. Back in grade five, we called ourselves "the guys." We used to say that we were smarter and tougher than all the other kids.

Then came the drugs and the parties. We did it all – together – daring each other to get higher and higher. And we stayed buddies, even after Matt went off to the preppie high school and I got stuck at Tech. Sure, he started moving with a new crowd, but we were still tight. Friends – right to the end – that was the old joke. And now this was the end.

I crushed out my smoke and was about to go home. That's when a black guy we called "Miami" came up to me.

"You hear what happened to Matt?" Miami asked. Then he answered his own question, "Somebody killed him."

"What are you talking about?" I shot back. "The guys say he OD'd, that's all."

"Sure, maybe he did," Miami said. "Maybe it was just an accident, but who gave him the pills – and why?"

Miami waited a second for his words to sink into my skull. "And how many more of us are going to bite the big one before we find out?"

I looked at Miami and just shook my head. I knew that Matt was really into drugs, more than any of us. I knew that Matt had been dealing more and more stuff. I knew he'd been trying to get his own connection to a big dealer. But I wasn't going to tell Miami all that.

Matt's death was an accident, that's all, I said to myself. That's what I was telling myself when the principal came out of the front doors. That's what I was thinking when the principal came over and grabbed me.

CHAPTER 2

A Chance to Get Even

The principal grabbed me by the arm, not rough, but hard enough that I could feel his fingers pressing into my skin.

"Kevin," he said, "I've got somebody inside who wants to see you."

"Who?" I asked, pulling my arm free.

"Just somebody in my office, waiting for you," he said. "Look, I know how you feel about your buddy Matt, but this isn't going to wait." The principal smiled at me, like he was really concerned about how I felt. Yeah, sure, that would be a first.

I just shrugged and followed him inside the office. He opened the door and I saw some lady sitting inside. She was dressed kind of casual, so I thought maybe she was a social worker. That's when the principal surprised me.

"Kevin," he said, "this is Detective Dugan from the police."

"Detective?" I asked, looking at her. She looked kind of cute for a cop – nice blonde hair, decent makeup, a pair of pretty tight jeans. I mean, if she were ten years younger and I were ten years older … but enough of that.

The detective must have seen me checking her out. "That's right, Kevin; not everybody on the drug squad is a man. Now pick your jaw off the floor and sit down," she said.

I turned back to the principal, but he had already gone. It was just the two of us – me and this lady cop. I sat down in one of the chairs and the cop got up and propped herself on the edge of the desk.

"Let me advise you that what you say can be used against you in court," Dugan began. "That you have the right to be rep — "

"I know my rights," I said, cutting her off. "But I haven't done nothing."

"Maybe not," she said, staring at me, "but I have a hunch you're not quite as clean as you pretend. Now where would something like this come from?" she asked. She reached into the pocket of her jacket and pulled out a dime of weed.

"I've never seen that before," I said.

"Really?" she replied, smiling because she could see right through me. "You sure you don't want a lawyer because this nice little baggie was sitting in your locker, Kevin. Now maybe somebody put it there to frame you. Maybe there are little drug elves out there who dropped off an early Christmas present. Or maybe some of your friends are turning on you, just like they turned on your buddy."

"I'm not a dealer," I told her. I was sweating now, sweating like crazy. Sure, I did a few drugs, but there was no way I should get nailed for this.

"I don't think you are, either," Dugan told me, putting the bag back in her pocket. "I just think you're just a kid who got into something over his head, just like your friend Matt. And I think you might be mad enough about what happened to your buddy that you might want to help us."

"Help you?" I said, laughing at her.

"Yes, help us get the guys who killed Matt. Matt was your friend, wasn't he?"

"The best," I said, looking down at my hands, remembering.

"That's what his mother said, too. She said that you'd gone to the party last night, together – 'the guys,' that's what you called yourselves. But you went home alive last night and your buddy Matt didn't. Somebody gave Matt Alcott some bad ecstasy, some killer ecstasy, then left him to die on the street. We found his body just off the bridge near McKnight Boulevard."

What was I supposed to say – that I was sorry? That I would have stopped Matt from taking the E if I could? That I didn't want my friend to die?

"Kevin, you know what I really hate about

being on the drug squad?" Dugan said to me. "It's telling parents that their kid is hooked on dope, an addict, a small-time dealer. The parents always give you this look, like you're lying or making it all up." Dugan waited for a second, shifting her legs on the desk. "And there's only one thing worse than telling them their kid is a junkie – and that's telling them that their kid is dead from an overdose.

"This morning," Dugan went on, "after they found the body, I had to go to tell Mrs. Alcott that her son was dead. She's a nice lady, Kevin, but I guess you already know that. She didn't believe me last year when I told her that Matt was hooked. She didn't believe me when I told her about the needle marks on his arms. Like most parents, she didn't know about that. But you did, didn't you?"

"Maybe," I whispered. There was something wrong with my voice, like I wanted to cry or something stupid like that.

"Kevin, I'm not here to try to nail you. I don't think you had much to do with Matt and his drug problem. And I don't think you gave him the drugs that killed him last night."

"No way I'd ever do that," I told her.

"But you were his friend, his best friend. You were at the party just before he died and you knew that Matt was shooting up. Still, you did nothing to help him – nothing to keep your best friend from getting killed."

That got to me. I jumped up from the chair, ready to reach out and strangle her. "Are you really blaming me?" I shouted at her.

She shook her head and stayed cool, so sure of herself.

"No, I think maybe you're blaming yourself right now. Matt's dead and it's too late to help him kick the habit, but you can still do something. You can help us find the people who killed your friend."

I stared out the window, clenching my fists while her words sunk in. Matt was dead and I was mad – madder than I'd ever been in my life. If the guy who gave him the killer dope had been in the room, I would have torn him apart with my bare hands. There was no way I'd let the killer go free.

"Give me a name, Kevin – give me something!" she begged.

"It had to be the Candyman," I said bitterly.

"The Candyman?" Dugan repeated.

"The big guy, where Matt was trying to make a connection. He's some kind of big dealer, that's all I know."

"It's not enough, Kevin. We need someone inside Matt's school, someone who can mix with the druggies and trace the drugs back to this Candyman guy."

"A narc," I said coldly.

"That's right. We need someone to go under cover at the high school, and maybe outside it. Somebody who can find out where the bad drugs are coming from, and then help us nail the guys on top," Dugan said. She stopped talking and stared at me.

"You don't mean *me*, do you?" I shot back.

"We need somebody who could fit in over there with the grade nine and ten kids," Dugan explained. "Somebody who knows about drugs. Somebody who looks like a drug user."

"You want *me* to be a narc?" I said. I knew I was shaking a little, maybe from anger, maybe from fear.

"Yeah," Dugan said, "that's pretty much what I had in mind."

"That stinks," I said.

"The whole thing stinks," Dugan said, reaching into her pocket for the dime she'd found in my locker. "You kids have got so much going for you. But you trash up your heads with this stuff – and worse, lots worse. Of course, I could always just bust you for this little package of weed, if you'd rather go that route."

"Don't threaten me," I told her. "I wouldn't turn on my friends just because some weed got found in my locker."

"I know you wouldn't," Dugan said. "The point is, you don't have to turn on your friends. We want the big guys – the Candyman and all his connections, right back to the lab. We want the guys who killed Matt."

"I won't do it," I told her, turning my face away.

"It's your choice, Kevin. But I wish you could have seen Mrs. Alcott this morning, and the look on her face. Or maybe if you'd have been with Matt when he died, on the street, alone …"

"Cut it out," I told her. I could see it in my mind – my best friend, dizzy and shaking, falling on the ground. Matt must have known he was dying even before the end came. He must have felt his heart racing, his teeth grinding, his breath coming in gasps. And what had I done to help him?

"It's too late for Matt – but you can still save

other kids. They don't deserve to die like that, Kevin."

"I've got to think," I mumbled.

"Sure," she said, "take the time you need to sort it out," she said, handing me a card. "This is a special number, so just ask for me when you make up your mind. Let me know which way it's going to be."

"You're just a —" and then I told her what I thought about her and all the other cops.

"I've heard what you kids think before, Kevin," she said, keeping her cool. "But it doesn't matter much if you like me or not. What matters is that your buddy Matt is dead and that more kids are going to die unless we get some help. Now think about that – and call me."

I nodded my head and walked out of the office, leaving Dugan there. Then I pushed into the first floor washroom and splashed some water on my face. There was a sick taste in my mouth that I tried to spit out.

I looked at myself in the one cracked mirror. First I saw my face, all crazy and strung out. Then

I saw Matt's face, but not like he used to be, more like a dead body, already rotting away.

I shook myself and pulled away from the mirror. Matt was dead and I was alive. What was I going to do now?

CHAPTER 3

Going Under Cover

I didn't make up my mind until the day of Matt's funeral. The service was supposed to be mostly for the family, but I went anyway. I just showed up at the church they had listed in the newspaper.

I sat in one of the back pews where I figured the family couldn't see me. I hadn't come to talk to them, anyway. I had come for Matt – to say goodbye, or maybe to say that I was sorry.

When it was all over, after they took the coffin

away and the family went out, I left the church. Outside, the cold wind whipped at my face. I pulled up my hood and was ready to go home when I felt somebody beside me.

"Man, that's pretty sad," I heard. I turned and saw that Miami had come up beside me.

"Yeah," I replied, trying to sound tough but my voice came out funny.

"I didn't know him like you did," Miami said. "But I don't like it when one of us goes down. It makes you want to know who did it, you know?"

I just nodded but didn't say anything. We were walking down the steps of the church, hiding our faces from the wind. Out front, they were putting the coffin inside a big black Caddy. I saw Matt's mother down there, dressed in black.

And she saw me.

For just a second, our eyes met. Just long enough for me to feel how bad it was for her – just long enough for me to see the question in her eyes. *How could you let this happen to my son?* That was the question.

I turned away. I didn't want to look at her or

Matt's two brothers or any of them. Part of me wanted to run off someplace, run and hide from myself. But another part wanted what she wanted – a chance to get back at whoever had killed Matt.

That was the part that won out. I took out Dugan's card, flipped it in my fingers, turned on my cellphone and dialed the number.

Two weeks later, I started my first day at Nelson – Matt's preppie high school. This is where he had made his connection, where he had got the drugs that killed him. Somebody here could lead me to the Candyman.

"What are you doing over with us?" Squeaky asked me.

I smiled and replied, "They kicked me over here 'cause I'm a brain, man. Just like the rest of you rocket scientists," is what I told him. But that was just the cover story. The truth was that I was a narc, I was working for the cops. The *real* truth was simpler still – I was after the Candyman.

Dugan had put the whole plan together. My going to Nelson was easy, since my principal at

Tech was glad to get rid of me. It was February, the start of the new term at both schools. Maybe ten kids moved from Nelson to my tech school, about five of us moved the other way. Besides, I really did have some brains – I just didn't want to do much with them.

So me changing schools was no big deal. I don't think Dugan even told my old principal that I was becoming a narc. And nobody at Nelson had a clue. Even when Dugan told my crazy old lady, she asked her to keep her mouth shut. It wasn't like I was a cop or I was going to be risking my life. I was just going in to get the goods on the Candyman – simple as that.

Dugan gave me a special number to call at the drug squad, and a code name. I was "Ricardo," just like Ricky Ricardo on the old TV show. Dugan wanted me to call in each day to let her know what was going down, or maybe to make sure I was still alive.

The phone in our house got a bug on it. Dugan thought she might get some evidence that way, but I told her the only evidence would be my old lady's friends. They'd be calling to play bingo. Dugan laughed, but the bug stayed on.

I remember the last thing Dugan said when the whole thing got set up. She told me, "Don't be a hero." I thought she was joking. I wanted to get the Candyman, I wanted to get even for Matt, but I sure didn't want to get killed while I was at it. My job was to come up with the evidence. Find the Candyman and come up with enough information to close him down.

There wasn't much action the first week at Nelson. I had enough trouble with the new classes and stuck-up kids. The Nelson teachers actually thought kids should *work* at learning stuff. They assigned *homework*, if you can believe that.

Of course, I kept my eyes open, but I wasn't looking too hard. Dugan had told me to go slow, not to push in too hard.

But the second week, I thought it was time to make a move. I knew Squeaky and some of the other hopheads from our parties. But either they didn't know much or they weren't talking. At least not to a guy from Tech.

Dugan said I should try to work in with a new group. I figured that made a lot more sense than batting zeros with the guys I knew. So at lunch that week, I started to hang around the parking lot. Nothing much at first. I went outdoors and off the school grounds, lit up a smoke, and just kept my eyes open.

There were some grade nine kids trying to look cool out there. They were puffing away on smokes, the way kids do when they're still learning how. A little smoking up and lots of giggles – that was all.

The real action was out in the cars, or off beyond the school. I knew Squeaky came out this way at lunch. I saw him meet with one guy I recognized from the party, Matt's last party. And there was a girl, too – a real nice-looking blonde whose name I didn't know. The first couple of days I spent outside – and it was real cold in February – I saw the bunch of them climb into a car. They'd climb out at the end of lunch, stoned but good. I guess the teachers at Nelson were so straight they couldn't tell.

I told Dugan on my cellphone.

"Sounds like you're on to something," she said to me. "Can you join them in the car?"

"Hey, it's not like you can go knock on the window and say I want in on the party," I told her.

"So what are you going to do?"

"I'm going to wait to get asked."

And that's what I did. I guess I could have told Squeaky that I needed to make a connection. But he knew I had plenty of connections at my old school. It would sound phony to say I was desperate to find a dealer. So I tried the next best thing.

"Hey, Squeaky, I want to meet that hot blonde," I told him.

"What hot blonde?" he said, as if he really didn't know.

"The one in the car, idiot. I've seen you guys out in the parking lot."

"Yeah, well, she's seen you smoking over by the fence," Squeaky told me.

"So tell me, what does she think?"

"She thinks all you guys from Tech are dirtbags."

"Tell her I'm not a dirtbag," I said to Squeaky. "Tell her it's real cold smoking outside and I've still got half a brick of black hash, if she's interested."

Squeaky just laughed and said, "Dawn needs your hash like I need a hole in my head. But I'll tell her you like her."

Then Squeaky was gone and I was left standing at my locker. So *Dawn* was her name, like the sun coming up in the morning, except that the look on her face wasn't very sunny. It seemed to me I had heard that name before, at a party someplace, but I couldn't nail it down.

It was a pretty nice name for a pretty hot chick – except she thought I was scum. All the preppies were like that. Just because I came from Tech, they acted like I had fleas crawling out of my leather jacket.

So I froze for a while more. I'd go out at lunch, grab a smoke and watch Dawn in the car. Squeaky and other guys came and went, but there was always Dawn. I could see her watching me, too, but not too much. Never more than a glance. I'd finish my smoke, swearing at her in my head for making me freeze my buns off. Then I'd stomp out the butt and go back inside.

It was stupid – I was getting no place – and that's what I told Dugan. But Dugan told me to cool down and see if I could move the action along. She wasn't going to bust the kids in the car for a few kilos of nothing. She wanted to get the big guy, the Candyman, and so did I.

So the next day I went over to Dawn's car, sat down on the edge of the hood, and smiled through the windshield right at her.

CHAPTER 4

Dawn and Her Friends

"All right, Kevin, get off my car," Dawn said to me. She was trying to be angry, but I knew there was a smile behind her eyes someplace.

"At least Squeaky told you my name," I said. Then I lit up a smoke and smiled at her and the other guys inside.

It worked – she smiled back. "Yeah, and he told me all about you. Now get off before I start this thing up and run you into the snow."

This blonde was no sweet little girl, but she didn't scare me. "It's cold smoking out here all by my lonesome," I told her.

"So open a door and come inside," she said, "but don't scrape the finish on my car." Then the window rolled up and I heard the guys inside the car laughing.

I went around to the other door and tried to open it, but it was locked. Dawn flicked the door lock switch and the locks popped up. As I climbed in back, I just kept on smiling.

Squeaky wasn't inside the car, and maybe that was just as well. In back, with me, there was a black kid named Jones who just stared out the window and kept quiet. In front was a guy from my English class named Cory, who looked real preppie, real straight.

Cory was smoking up, Jones seemed to be on downers, and Dawn was just looking at me.

"I like your brand of smokes," I told Cory, sniffing at the smell of the joint. "But don't you worry about getting caught?"

"The teachers are blind," Cory told me. "Besides,

I'm on the student council drug advisory group. I tell all the niners how bad it is to smoke up, how it destroys your brains."

Jones seemed to wake up at that comment and gave a smile to the kids in front. "I always wondered what happened to your brains, man."

"Shut up, yo-yo," Cory yelled, though Dawn and I were laughing, too. "So, I tell the niners that drugs will destroy their little lives. I play the game and the principal loves me," he said, taking a toke and passing the joint to Dawn.

Dawn took a drag and passed it back, holding

the smoke in. I noticed that neither of them offered me any, so I took out a smoke of my own.

"Is that all you brought?" Dawn asked, looking down at my cigarettes.

"That's all I *carry*," I told her. "Maybe you Nelson guys can get away with getting baked at lunch, but at Tech the teachers can smell it a mile away."

"So why did you come over here to preppie-land?" she asked, staring at me while Cory copped the joint.

"Maybe I wanted to meet you," I said in my Barry White kind of voice.

"Oh, this guy is smooooth," Jones said. "He's one smooth dude."

"You were Matt Alcott's friend," Cory said, handing the joint back to Dawn.

"Yeah," I replied, getting a little nervous. I felt like I was being tested for something, checked out to see if I might be dangerous.

"We kind of wondered if you were out to get even with somebody," Cory went on.

For a second I didn't know what to say. It was

almost as if these guys had me pegged already, so I decided to play dumb. "Get who, man?" I asked him. "Matt OD'd and he's gone. There's nothing anybody can do for him now and there wasn't anything I could do for him back then. You know what they say – life goes on."

"I told you," Cory said to Dawn. "Squeaky said that he's over it."

"Squeaky also said you've got a brick," Dawn said, turning to me. From the look on her face, I had a hunch that she still didn't trust me.

"Maybe I've got what's *left* of a brick," I told her. "But I only share what I've got with friends – good friends."

"Aren't we your friends?" Jones spoke up. "I mean, we're keeping you warm in this truly excellent vehicle, are we not?"

"Yeah, and you're letting me watch you guys bogart a joint," I said sharply. "Thanks for all the excitement, friend."

"We were just wondering," Dawn spoke up, "if maybe you were thinking of dealing around here – not much, but a little."

"I'm not a dealer," I said to her, smiling again. *Show her those pearly white teeth and maybe she'll trust you,* I said to myself.

"That's good," Cory told me, "because we don't need any more dealers at Nelson. We thought you aimed to pick up where Matt left off."

"Matt left off dead," I told them.

"So could you," Dawn said, as simple as if she were talking about the weather. "Don't butt in where you don't belong."

Jones thought that this exchange was real funny. He started giggling so hard I wanted to belt him, but that would have blown the whole thing.

I sat there quietly, trying to keep myself under control. At least now I knew why it had taken so long to get where I was. These guys thought I was moving in on their turf. They thought I'd come over to push drugs, maybe take over business at the whole school. Now they were testing me out to make sure I was no threat.

And what if I passed the test?

"You want some of this, Kevin?" Dawn asked me. There was a little less edge in her voice now, and a nice kind of look in her eyes.

"Not now," I told her. "Got a math test coming up and need to have most of my brain working for it. Maybe just one drag," I said, copping the joint.

That got Jones giggling again and even brought a smile to Cory's face.

"Sorry, to leave you out in the cold so long, but we wanted to check," Dawn said. "Somebody said you might try moving in here, taking over."

"Somebody's a jerk," I told her.

"And there's a rumour going around that the cops have got a guy working for them," Cory said.

Don't freeze up, I told myself, *don't even blink. Stay cool*. "You think I look like a narc?" I shot back at him. I said it like I was really insulted, like I would slug him if he said it again.

"Well, we had to check you out," Dawn said.

"You like what you see?" I asked her, giving her that toothy smile.

"I don't like anything … ever," she said, opening the door to the car.

"Dawn, you are such a downer," Cory told her. "We'll party tomorrow and see if it brightens you up a little."

"What about me?" I asked.

"It depends," Cory said, nodding at Dawn.

Dawn didn't say a word, but something about the way she looked at me told me that I was in. Their next party would include me, too – and it would get me a little closer to the Candyman.

CHAPTER 5

The Connection

Dugan was very excited when I called her on my cellphone. "So you made a connection."

"Yeah, but I'm going to need some money. At least enough cash to buy an ounce or two," I told her.

"I'll get you the money when you're ready for it," Dugan said. "But we might be ready to move in before then."

"You just don't trust me with the cash," I

laughed.

"A month ago I wouldn't trust you with one red cent," Dugan told me. "Now I just said I'll get you what you need. Just remember, Kevin, the higher up you go, the more careful you've got to be."

"I'm always careful," I told her and hit the off button.

I had always been more careful than Matt. I stayed away from the hard stuff and the drugs that really wasted you. I never did shrooms the way Matt did because I didn't see weird bugs crawling under my skin as my idea of a good time. And there was too much that could go wrong with pills. You never really knew what kind of stuff the pusher had sold you. Besides, you had to deal with a real heavy-duty crowd to get it. That's what Matt didn't think about and maybe that's why he died.

I took about a quarter of the hashish I had left and wrapped it in foil. It was like my mother had made me a little brownie for school. Then I hid it in the bottom of my gym bag. It was my ticket into the group. I just wondered how many more tickets I'd have to buy to get all the way to the Candyman.

The party was after school at Cory's house, a big ranch-style house not far from school. His parents were both lawyers and were always off someplace making the money that kept Cory in dope.

Pretty strange, I thought when I came up to Cory's house. Why would some rich kid like Cory end up a junkie? Or a girl like Dawn? She had looks, money, a car – and a big bad drug habit that she couldn't control. I wondered if she was shooting up, but you couldn't tell with the long sleeves she always wore.

There were only six of us at the party – Dawn, Cory, Squeaky, Jones, a stoned girl named Sara and me. Cory took us down to this enormous family room. Then he put some videos on a screen that seemed to take up a whole wall.

Cory turned to me while the others paired off. "You bring some of your stash?" he asked me, his voice suddenly cold as ice.

"Just like I promised," I said, taking the hash from my bag and tossing it to him.

I looked up and caught Dawn smiling at me, though she looked away when I caught her eye.

Cory cut the hash into pieces and put one piece into a pipe. Then he lit his lighter and held it under the bowl. He passed the pipe after he took a hit.

I noticed that while everyone else was smoking up, Dawn ducked upstairs. When she came back down to the family, she was high on something. She had that kind of blissed-out look – not happy – but sort of mellow.

"You want some?" I asked, offering her the hash pipe.

"Don't need it," she told me as she brushed the blonde hair back out of her face.

"You know, when you smile, it just rips me up," I said – and that wasn't just a line.

"I'll stop smiling if it hurts that bad," she replied, leaning into my shoulder.

"I can handle it," I told her. "Since Matt died I think I can handle almost anything."

"You were close?"

I nodded and looked away, thinking about the night Matt died on the street.

"Me, too," she said, touching my arm.

I turned back with a question in my eyes. "Not

like you're thinking," she explained quickly. "But I liked Matt and I heard him talk about you a lot. It's real sad, what happened," she said, her eyes turning down.

"You know, since Matt's gone I've had some trouble getting supplies," I told her. "He used to keep me stocked up and I looked after some of the other guys at Tech."

"You said you weren't a dealer."

"I'm not," I told her. "I'm not even a pusher, but sometimes I'll make a connection so I can share with my friends, if you know what I mean."

"What do you need?" Dawn asked me. She had a bored look on her face, like she had this kind of talk far too often.

"Some weed – one ounce, and a little E, maybe ten or fifteen tabs," I told her.

She did some mental math and then gave me her price. "Bring me the money on Monday and I'll take care of it," Dawn told me.

"Hey, you can move pretty fast," I told her, putting my arm around her shoulders.

"Only drugs," Dawn replied, "so don't get any

ideas."

"Hey, I'm a shy guy," I told her, though we both knew that wasn't the truth. "But, you know, if you've got a good supply, I could maybe get rid of some other stuff."

"Like what?" Dawn asked me, her voice all flat, ready for business.

"Like some heroin – at the right price, I could get rid of a few hits in no time," I told her.

"Over at Tech?" she asked, raising her eyebrows. "Those guys are still on weed and can't afford much else."

"Well, I'm just saying – "

"And I'm saying don't try moving in here," Dawn said, cold as ice all of a sudden. She looked over at the TV, where Cory had his arm around Sara, then got up and walked over to talk to him. I was left standing by myself, wondering if I was pushing too hard, too fast. Dugan had said I should go slowly, and here I was offering to push smack to the Tech kids. Maybe I should take a couple lessons in how to listen.

Squeaky Brown came over to talk, but the guy

had been a real zero for me ever since I moved to Nelson. I left him, just like Dawn left me, and sat down to watch the DVDs. There was still plenty of hash for the pipe, enough to keep me wasted for hours.

That's what I did when the pressure got to me. Maybe that's what these preppies did, too. We were all hiding out from some problem out there, some screw-up in our lives. At least I knew what mine was, and she was sitting at home, ready to drive me nuts when I got in the door. But I wondered about Dawn and what kind of screw-up turned a girl with everything into a junkie.

I guess I spent a lot of time sitting alone, thinking about all this stuff. When I started coming down, it was way past dinner. I figured I'd better clear out before my old lady had a heart attack. I said goodbye to Cory and the others, then found my coat. It wasn't until I was ready to leave that Dawn came up to me.

"Hey, Kevin, were you serious about the hard candy?" Dawn asked me, her voice all warm and friendly.

I nodded.

"Then somebody wants to meet you," she said to me, as if that should mean something.

"Somebody who?" I replied, too baked to make sense of it.

"Somebody who might have what you want … maybe next week some time. Get some cash ready and we'll see what happens."

"Can't you handle it yourself?" I asked. I wondered what level of dealing she could handle.

"Not me – just somebody. But the big man needs some time to check you out," she said. And that was all I got from her before she pushed me out the door.

CHAPTER 6

Nobody Can Help

I asked Dugan for five hundred bucks, and she got it dropped off in a day. I figured it would look funny if I had too much money. I mean, where would a kid from Tech get really big cash unless I was already dealing.

On Monday, Dawn told me the deal was on, but I had to wait the rest of the week for Dawn to take me to her connection. As each day passed, I got more nervous.

"Anything yet?" Dugan asked when I called in.

"Nothing," I told her.

"Your friend Dawn has got a pretty little rap sheet," Dugan told me. "She's not the sweet blonde kid that she seems."

"Yeah, I kind of figured that," I mumbled.

When somebody tapped me in the hall on Friday, I jumped. But it was only Dawn, smiling, asking me if I had the cash. When I said yes, she said she'd drive me to see "somebody" after school.

I was nervous as anything, sitting in Dawn's

car. She pulled out of the parking lot and onto 4th Street, then drove downtown. I pulled out a smoke and tried to act cool, all the while my insides were twisting up.

"Who is this *somebody?*" I asked her.

"My cousin," she said, zipping the wheel to the right, checking in the mirror. It was almost as if she thought we were being followed, and maybe we were. Dugan said that she was going to keep an eye on me.

"Your cousin have a name?" I asked her.

"Buddy," she said, checking the mirror again.

Dawn seemed to be as nervous as I was – and that was plenty nervous. I wondered whether I could really handle this or not.

I had heard about Buddy from Matt maybe a year ago. He was Matt's connection to somebody big, maybe to the Candyman himself. So Buddy was kind of a halfway stop on the trip I wanted to make.

We got to an apartment parking lot on 1st Street and Dawn pulled the car into a space. The building was nothing special, just your average high-rise. I followed Dawn into the building and watched while she pressed the button marked "B. Carman." I noticed her hand was shaking.

The guy who met us didn't look at all like Dawn. He had long, dark hair, big eyebrows and an earring in one ear. He looked almost as ugly as Dawn was beautiful, so if he really was her cousin then somebody got switched at birth.

I followed Buddy inside, wondering if there'd be guys waiting to jump me when we got to the living room. But it was just us – and Buddy wanted to test me.

"So you've got friends at Tech," he said, sitting back on the couch.

"I've got friends all over," I replied. I noticed that Dawn had gone off to some other room and left the two of us alone.

"Who wants the smack?" he said.

"Who wants to know?" I tossed back at him, then lit up a smoke.

"I'm Buddy," he said, smiling for the first time, "and I knew Matt."

"We all did," I told him, trying to keep my hand

from shaking. "Dawn tells me that you've got what I need."

"Maybe," Buddy said, looking off to the bedroom. "But first I want to know where the stuff is going. You kids don't seem to get this, but there are guys who get upset when you move into their area."

"I'm dealing to a kid named Birney," I said, looking away to cover the lie. "I don't know where it's going to end up after him, and I don't really care."

"You should, Kevin," Buddy replied. He sounded like an old man though he was only about thirty. "In this business, you try to find out everything or you end up like your friend Matt."

"I'm not in the business," I told him. "I'm just trying to make a buck to keep myself going for a while. And I like to keep my friends happy – that's all."

"That's good enough for small time," Buddy told me. "You brought some cash?"

"Five hundred."

"Five hundred for all the stuff you want?"

Buddy said, his big eyebrows lifting up. "You think this is some kind of charity I'm running?"

"Five hundred now, five hundred *after* I get the stuff," I told him.

"Fair enough," he muttered.

"I told Dawn I needed a *good* price, not the kind of deal I can get from a street pusher," I said.

"Done," he said, staring at me. "Give me five hundred now, get the rest to Dawn right after delivery. You'll get a phone call telling you where to pick it up."

"You trust Dawn with the money but not with the stuff, eh?" I wondered if she could hear me in the other room.

"I don't trust anybody – and that includes you, smart face," Buddy said.

"Dawn told me you're her cousin," I said, "but I've got my doubts. You got some other interest in the girl?" I asked.

"I don't mess with junkies," Buddy said, pulling a joint out of a box next to the couch. "She really is my cousin, you know. You like her, go ahead and go for it. I won't stop you. But I warn you, man, what you see isn't what you get."

At that point, Dawn came out from some other room. I could tell by the way she walked that she was really amped. She must have been popping something while Buddy and I were talking.

Buddy took one look at her and shook his head. "You drive her home, okay?" he said, passing me the joint. "She's messed up enough without her trying to drive like that."

So I drove Dawn to her house, a place out by Elbow Park with a garage as big as my mom's apartment. She was coming down pretty bad by then, talking to herself about how rotten life was. I tried to lighten her up, but it wasn't working. By the time we got to her place, she was crying. The crying got worse as she talked about her parents, the way they pushed her to get top marks. The way she could never measure up. I felt bad for her and tried to put my arm around her, but she pushed me away.

"I just want to help," I told her.

"Nobody can help me," she said, sniffling. Then she wiped her face and went off to the big house at the end of a long driveway.

CHAPTER 7

A Wire … or Not

I guess I should have known things were heating up when Dugan said she wanted to see me. I called to tell her about Buddy and the deal. I didn't really need anything else from her, but Dugan was worried. She wanted to see me first.

We met at a restaurant downtown. Dugan said she didn't want to be seen coming to my house. I thought all this secret meeting stuff was a bit much, but Dugan wouldn't listen.

I was drinking a Dr Pepper when Dugan came in. At first, I hardly knew who she was. She was dressed in some jeans, a pair of boots and a tight-fitting top.

"Hey, you look like a pretty hot babe," I said, grinning at her.

She just frowned at me and slid quickly into the booth. "I try to fake it, sometimes," she said. Dugan gave a quick look around the quiet restaurant, then sat back and ordered coffee.

"We ran a check on Buddy," she said, "but didn't come up with much. He can't be very big in the Candyman's set-up."

"I'd guess he's just a local dealer, maybe with a habit," I told her. "From what he says, he needs money pretty fast. But I guess he has to check with his source for any kind of big deal."

"We're going to be putting a bug on his car," Dugan told me. "Once we can trace him back to the Candyman, we can close the whole thing down."

"Just a reminder – I'm not going to take the stand against my friends," I said.

"I know that," Dugan answered. "But Buddy

was no friend of yours – or Matt's – and the Candyman gave him the drugs that –"

Just then, the outside door opened. Dugan shut up and looked like she didn't know me. She held up some papers that almost hid her face.

After a minute, she must have figured it was safe to go ahead. "It all depends on how much stuff we find when we bust them. If the apartment is clean, we'll need your help to prove he's a dealer."

"Yeah, well, I was just wondering ..." I began.

"What about?" Dugan asked.

"You see, there's this girl …" I said, my voice falling off.

"Dawn – am I guessing right?"

"Yeah, she's Buddy's cousin, but she's not in this real deep."

"You told me she was a dealer at Nelson, and a junkie," Dugan replied.

The outside door opened again and this time I looked up. I think we were both getting nervous. Again, it was nobody.

"Listen, I just don't want the courts coming down on her," I told Dugan. "I said I'd help you get the guys who killed Matt, so I'll go to court against the Candyman. But I won't say anything against Dawn – you got me?"

"Have you fallen for a junkie, Kevin?" Dugan asked. She was smiling at me as if I'd gone right out of my mind.

I could feel my cheeks glowing as I answered her. "I haven't fallen for anybody. The thing is, I think she's got some problems, personal problems, and that's why she's pushing for Buddy. She's not a big dealer, just a kid who needs some help."

"You want her in a drug program?" Dugan asked me.

"I just don't want her to go to jail, that's all."

"I'll do something if I can, Kevin, but you watch yourself. It's really hard to break junkies from the habit. It isn't the pills or the heroin that gets them hooked, it's some problem in their heads. Even if they can get off the drugs, they're still messed up upstairs," she said, tapping her forehead. Then Dugan shook her head and added, "You know, I'm starting to sound like a mother."

"You're not old enough to be my mother," I told her, thinking of my old lady.

"But I am worried about you getting in over your head," Dugan went on. "When you go to Buddy's place, you're going to be in real danger."

"I can look after myself," I said.

"Don't give me stupid lines out of movies," Dugan snapped back. "You're not dealing with street pushers any more. Buddy might be the guy who killed Matt. We don't know yet, but if he did, all your tough words won't do much for you. This is big time, Kevin. The Candyman would kill you or me without a second thought, and maybe Buddy would, too."

"So you want me to back off?" I said.

"No, I want you to wear this," she said quietly. "Reach under the table and take what I give you, but just slip it into your pocket. Don't even look at it until later."

I did what she said, reaching under the table for Dugan's hand. She gave me something that felt like a piece of wire.

"Can I bend it?" I asked her.

"Just don't break it in half," she replied. "These wires cost a month's pay. When you go to Buddy's, I want you to put the wire under the collar of your shirt. Then call me on your cellphone so I can get someone to listen in. But you've got to call or the wire won't listen in to anything."

"I'm glad about that," I told her. I could just imagine this guy listening to my old lady nagging me to stay out of trouble. Or me going to the john.

"One other thing – make sure I get all the drugs after you pick them up," she said.

"Don't I even get a piece of it?" I said, grinning at her.

"Don't joke around," Dugan snapped back. She looked around the room one more time. "You're in this a long way now, and that took a lot of guts. Don't get cocky just because you've been lucky so far. And wear the wire. If you get in trouble, we'll know and find a way to get you out of it. If not ..."

"I'm on my own," I finished for her.

CHAPTER 8

Buddy and the Candyman

Over the next two weeks, I started to think Dugan was just crazy. Everything was so easy. None of them suspected, not even Dawn, and we were getting pretty close to the Candyman.

I met Dawn and picked up the heroin, ecstasy and weed where I was told. It was taped under the sink in the washroom of the Mr. Burger joint on Macleod Trail.

When I gave Dugan the drugs, she said I'd have

to do a bigger deal to get close to the top guys. So I waited. For now, I didn't care. I was spending lots of time with Dawn, in her car, after school at her house, anywhere we could find to be alone. Maybe Dugan was right – maybe I was falling for her.

So I wasn't thinking much about drugs or the Candyman when Dawn called me just before the March break. I figured she wanted to talk. We'd been talking a lot, about her habit, about how she'd tried to kick it, about how she was going to try again. We talked about our screwed-up families, too. We talked about everything – except what I was *really* doing at Nelson. I couldn't tell her that I was a narc, working undercover to bust her cousin. Somehow, I thought, after the bust, after she had kicked the habit . . . .

So, I should have known from her voice when she called. I should have had a hint that it would be trouble.

It was late, almost midnight, and she said she just *had* to see me. Sure, I told her, and got ready to be picked up. Twice before we'd gone out like this – she'd be coming down from a high and have to talk. So I'd go out with her, hold her hand a little, buy her a coffee, and that would be that.

This time I met her outside my house and I could see right away that she was real strung. I climbed into the car beside her and asked the question.

"What's the matter?"

"It's Buddy," she answered. "He wants to see you, like right away."

I did a quick double take as Dawn pulled away from the curb. I wasn't ready to handle this. The wire was sitting back in my bedroom, neatly hidden in the closet. Even if I could find a way to call in, the cops would have no way to listen. It was like I said to Dugan – I was on my own.

"I thought *you* wanted to talk," I said, twisting in my seat. "I'm not into seeing Buddy this late – I've got school tomorrow."

"He told me to bring you," Dawn said, almost like a robot. She was sniffling, like she was trying to hold back some real tears.

"You okay?" I asked her, reaching out to touch her hand on the shift lever.

"Yes … no … oh, I don't know," Dawn snapped at me.

Before I could get any more out of her, we were parked outside Buddy's high-rise. Even as we went up the elevator, I knew something was wrong with all this. If I'd had half a brain, I would have taken off right then. But if I did that, then Dawn might get into trouble and I knew how bad that trouble could be.

Buddy was waiting for us at the door. "Come on in, Kevin," he said, smiling like he was my best friend.

I nodded grimly and walked into the living room. There were two guys sitting there: one was older, with greying hair, sort of a cool dude but a little too old to pull it off. The other guy was younger, a real greaser with slicked-back hair and pockmarked skin.

"I think you've been wanting to meet somebody," Buddy said, pointing to the old grey-haired man. "Kevin, this is the Candyman."

The whole thing went through my head real quick. *They knew it all. I was caught, and I might as*

well be dead.

The greaser moved behind me, blocking the way out. Dawn was off in a corner, crying now, shaking like an addict coming down off the big horse.

"Search him," the Candyman snapped. His voice was tough and cold, like somebody who's used to giving orders.

The greaser came up behind me and checked me over. He even checked the collar of my shirt for a wire – the wire I wished I had.

"He's clean," the meatball said, pushing me forward into a chair.

"Kevin, who are you working for?" Buddy asked me.

"I'm not working for anybody," I told them, trying to stay cool. I tried to look like I didn't know what they were talking about.

"You should have known the kid was a plant," the Candyman said to Buddy. "He's a friend of that kid who died and you treat him like he's your long-lost brother. Talk about stupid, Buddy, you take some kind of prize."

"Look, I found out in time, didn't I?" Buddy said. He seemed almost as scared as I was.

"You working for the cops, kid?" the Candyman said to me. "You know who planted the bug on Buddy's car?"

"I don't know nothing," I pleaded. "Look, you got some problem with Buddy, it doesn't have anything to do with me. I did a little deal with him, that's all. Just let us out of here and you do what you want." I was shaking almost as bad as Dawn

was, and I wasn't coming down off a high.

"Nice try, Kevin, but it won't work," Buddy said to me. "We checked for your friend Birney and he says he never bought that smack from you. He says he never bought anything from you," Buddy said. Then he came over and grabbed me by the neck, pulling me up off the chair. "Now what's the real story?"

"Birney's lying," I gasped, trying to find breath while Buddy held my neck. "He asked me to make the deal and get him the heroin – I swear it."

"And Birney swears that *he's* telling the truth," Buddy spat in my face. "You're the guy who doesn't add up, Kevin. You come over from Tech, move in on Dawn, make some phony deal with me and then there's a bug on my car."

"It all stinks, kid," answered the Candyman. "But maybe you'll open up when you see what comes next. Come on, we're all going for a ride."

The big greaser was behind me, a gun in his hand all of a sudden. I looked over at Dawn, but she was in no shape to help anybody.

"Are you going to kill me like you did Matt?" I

asked. I wanted to know, even if I could never tell anyone else.

"Sort of," Buddy said, smiling at me, "except your friend swallowed all those pills on his own. You've got some stuff to tell us first, before we figure what to do with you."

"So you're going to kill me, just like that?"

None of them answered. Buddy grabbed Dawn, who was shaking and crying like crazy. The meatball grabbed me with one hand and held his gun with the other. I could feel the cold steel of the gun barrel pressed into my back.

CHAPTER 9

"You Gotta Do Something!"

The elevator doors opened to the underground garage. The big greaser had my arm twisted behind me. Maybe I could pull free, but what then? If I ran for it, they would just chase me down, or the thug would shoot me. Even if I made it, they'd still have Dawn with them. But I felt stupid feeling like that – after what that junkie had done to me.

"Over there," the Candyman said, pointing to the far wall.

The greaser pushed me forward before I was ready. I stumbled and started to fall, but he held my arm tight.

"Kevin," I heard. It was Dawn, her eyes suddenly open, looking right at me.

For a second, I was angry. Why had she just been standing like a zombie all this time? But then I saw through it – maybe she was just waiting for a chance when we could run for it, maybe she had some kind of plan.

"Come on, kid, I'm not about to drag you," the greaser said, twisting my arm a little more.

"Easy on the bruises," the Candyman said. "It's got to look like an overdose."

The five of us began moving past the first row of parked cars. When we got a little beyond them, Buddy held back, then told the others to stop.

"Something's wrong," Buddy said. "I see some lights –" But Buddy didn't get a chance to finish.

"Police, hold it right there!" The words rang out through the parking garage.

I never thought there'd be a day when I'd be happy to see the cops – but this was it. They must have picked up Dawn's call with the bug on my house phone. Now if only they could get us out of here.

Everything began to move real fast. Buddy grabbed Dawn and pulled her in front of him, like a shield. The greaser pulled me back, tight against him, and the Candyman got back behind us so I was a shield for both of them. It was my body that would take the bullets if shooting started.

"We got the kids," the Candyman shouted out to the cops. I could smell the stink of his breath as he screamed out behind my ear.

The cop's voice came out of the darkness. It was as cool and controlled as they seem on TV. "Put your guns down and come forward with your hands over your heads!"

Buddy swore and then yelled, "You're going to let us out of here or these kids are taking some bullets."

I looked over at Dawn. She was scared white by fear, or by Buddy squeezing her neck. I also saw that Buddy didn't have a gun. The only gun aimed at us was the one the greaser had pointed at my head.

"Don't risk a murder charge," the cop's voice said back. "Throw down your guns and let the kids go."

"No way," the Candyman shouted out. "We're going over to my car and getting inside, real slow and real peaceful. You just keep your distance and the kids will be okay, but if you cops try one move, then the boy gets it first."

"You'll never get out of here alive," I muttered to the Candyman.

"You better pray that I do, 'cause you're going to be dead first," he spat back at me. "Now let's move."

Buddy and Dawn came beside us so the five of us were together again, with me dead centre. We moved forward slowly, like some monster with ten legs. The cops didn't seem to know what to do with us. It was as if each side was waiting for the other one to make some mistake.

I caught Dawn's eye. She looked back at me for a second, then looked down. Buddy had his arm around her waist now, holding her tight. We had made it half way to a white Jaguar parked by the far wall. Another minute and we'd be inside it and then anything could happen.

I figured my chances of ending up dead got better with every step we took. All I could do was hope that the cops figured the same way in case we got a chance to run for it.

Then it all broke loose. "Kevin!" Dawn yelled to me. At the same time, she jabbed her elbow into Buddy's ribs and reached over to grab the greaser's gun.

I bent over so the big guy wasn't right at my skull, then jammed my elbow into him. The thug let out a grunt, letting go his grip on my other wrist. I pulled free and elbowed him again.

Somehow – I'll never know how – the gun went off. There was only one shot at first, but then I heard a couple more shots before Dawn screamed.

It was all so confused. I didn't know who was shooting at what, so I grabbed Dawn and just fell on top of her.

I lay there, covering Dawn, waiting for the next shot to come screaming through me. It would get me first, because I was Dawn's shield now. I kept praying that the cops would move fast. It was all up to them – and it seemed to take forever. All I could do was lie there, waiting for a bullet to jam into my spine.

Then I heard one gunshot, and another. I waited, tensed, for the shot that would go into me, but that shot never came. I felt a spray of blood from above me, and then the body of the greaser fell on top of us.

Up above, there was screaming and yelling from all over. The Candyman was yelling, "Don't shoot!" The cops were telling everyone to put their arms up over their heads. It seemed like everybody was yelling and going crazy.

Then I heard a voice I knew, just over my head. "Kevin, did you get hit?" Dugan said.

The iron smell of blood was everywhere, and I felt like I was going to be sick. Two cops pulled the greaser's body off me so I could sit up.

Dugan was staring at me. "Kevin, there's blood all over your shirt."

And then we both looked down at Dawn. The

blood on my shirt was hers, from a hole in her side as big as my fist. Dawn wasn't screaming or crying or moving. The only thing moving in the whole world was her blood, bubbling onto the floor.

"Do something!" I screamed at the cops. "You gotta do something!"

CHAPTER 10

Friends to the End

Dawn took a long time to recover from being shot. The greaser's bullet went through her thigh, shattered her hip bone, and came out the back. For a while, after the doctors did what they could, we still didn't know if she would make it. That was the worst part.

After that, her recovery was just slow. She was in the hospital for two weeks, then back home for two months. And I was with her every day.

I suppose there was one good side to all this. Dawn kicked her habit. She'd been into heroin – mainlining it – and that habit kept her tied to Buddy. But the time she spent in bed getting over the bullet was also time spent kicking the habit. By June she was healed up from both of them. And the two of us, well, we're still together. Maybe that means something, eh?

The shootout really busted up the Candyman's whole drug ring. The greaser died that night, and maybe I should feel bad about that, but I don't. He had it coming. And so does Buddy, killing Matt and hooking his cousin on smack. Buddy will be sent up for a long time when it all comes out in court. The Candyman will maybe get seven years for his part. The big guys never seem to pay as much as the small pushers, but at least he's out of the business.

Dugan is pretty much out of the cop business after what happened. The brass didn't like the way she used me in the Candyman case, so she's been sent to desk work. I guess the cops won't be using kids as narcs any more.

Not that Dugan cares too much. It turns out she was pregnant all that time we worked to find the Candyman. Right now, she's big as a house. It looks like twins in October, she told me. What could I say? I always thought she was too nice to be a cop.

The other day, I stopped off to see Matt's mother. I didn't say much, just that I was sorry about how he died. Maybe I could have told her how I helped close down the Candyman, but I kept my mouth shut. My name never came out in the papers. It was better that way. Right now, only Dawn and I know what happened that night – and we aren't talking.

I don't think Mrs. Alcott would even care about all that. She seemed glad to see me, glad to have somebody to talk to. She blamed the drugs for killing her son – and she was right about that – and blamed herself, too. I tried to tell her that sometimes things just happen. Sometimes you get caught up in stuff over your head. Maybe she even heard what I said, I don't know.

But when I left Matt's house, I felt good. I'd done what I had to do for my friend. We'd been friends right to the end – and even a little after that.

This book is dedicated to the real Kevin,
who helped with all the details, and was
smart enough to get straight.

Here are some other titles you might enjoy:

Our Plane Is Down
by DOUG PATON

A small plane goes down in the bush, hours from anywhere. The radio is broken, the pilot is out cold. There's only a little water and even less food. Can Cal make it through the woods to save his sister, the pilot and himself?

The Kid Is Lost
by PAUL KROPP

It's a babysitter's worst nightmare: a child goes missing! Kurt has to get help and lead the search into a deadly swamp on his ATV. Will he find the lost child in time?

My Broken Family
by **PAUL KROPP**

Divorce is always rotten. When Maddy's parents split up, her whole life starts to fall apart. Maddy holds on to her dancing as one thing that is really hers. But when it's all over, she finds that love is stronger than she thought.

Scarface by **PAUL KROPP**

Coming to the United States had been a great thing for Tranh. This was a country of peace and wealth and happiness. So why did Martin Beamis keep picking on him? Did this rich kid have nothing better to do than make life rotten for someone who had already suffered so much?

Dark Ryder
by LIZ BROWN

Kate Hanson finally gets the horse of her dreams, but Dark Ryder comes with a catch. Kate has just three months to turn him into a winner, or she'll lose her horse forever.

Terror 9/11 by DOUG PATON

Seventeen-year-old Jason was just picking up his sister at the World Trade Centre when the first plane hit. As the towers burst into flames, he has to struggle to save his sister, his dad and himself.